The
ALPHA

Katherine Zartman

Lavender Moon Publishing

CHAPTER ONE

Spring has finally arrived, and I decide to take a drive in the mountains. I will check to be sure Independence Pass is open, as I live just outside of Aspen.

I am anxious to see the blooms of wildflowers and columbines high up in the mountains. It is a Tuesday, so Independence Pass should be pretty free of traffic. No Winnebagos to halt my ascent and no backing down to a wider area, always a possibility on the very narrow road.

The car is gassed up, tires are good, granola bars and cold water are in the car. I grab a hoodie and a jacket; you never know in Colorado. I stop at one of the few turnouts and carefully make my way down to the river. Cold and clear, a few patches of snow still cling to the riverbank and I inhale the scent of pines and wet earth.

I am so enjoying the drive, the car stereo turned up, window down and Marty Robbins belting out a soulful ballad.

I notice a few signs announcing a veterinary clinic and wolf rescue just a few miles ahead as I descend from the pass. Wolves? I decide to stop and see the rescue of these premier predators. The small sign in tucked under a large blue spruce so I almost miss the dirt driveway.

I pull in and observe a couple talking to a tall man dressed in tight jeans and a blue flannel shirt. Just beyond a wire fence are several gray and white wolves; they are watching the man in the flannel. I open my car door and the eyes turn to me as if to say, "Lunch!"

Flannel Shirt comes over and extends his hand. "Welcome, I'm Dr. Taylor." I shake his rough, calloused hand and notice scars on it, and his forearm.

"Glad to meet you, Dr. Taylor. My name is Annie. I hope I'm not interrupting anything." I can't help but notice his two enormous green eyes gazing down at me from his rugged, clean shaven face.

I turn my gaze toward the sound of snarls coming from the canines behind him. Dr. Taylor says something to the pack, and it sounds just like the snarls from the wolves.

"What can I do for you, Annie?" I hesitate to answer as a frisson of fear runs through me. Swallowing the fear, I tell him, "I was curious to see the wolves." He smiles and reaches out to my elbow, which produces more snarls and a resounding response from him. We walk over to the fence line and the couple thanks him and says goodbye. I turn to him and ask him to tell me about the rescue. He pulls my arm again, which draws more snarls from the fence, and he says, "Come, we need to get away from the pack; they don't want me near you."

We move to a nearby fallen tree and sit down. I ask him what he means, and he patiently explains that the pack considers him an Alpha, leader. "I provide them with food and take care of them as an alpha of their kind would do. It's complicated."

We talk for forty-five minutes and he tells me how the rescue started and how many wolves are here: four females and two young males. He hunts food for them, as do other hunters who occasionally bring deer and rabbit for the pack. I am fascinated as he tells me about rescue life, quickly directing me to call him just Taylor, so I follow his direction. He tells me not to move, as it is feeding day for the pack. He ambles over to a large cooler and extracts bloody meat, still bearing hair, and goes to the fence. Six sets of eyes watch every move and bare gleaming white teeth in anticipation. He throws the food over the fence and the pack instantly races for the only meal of the day.

We watch for several minutes and then he grabs my hand. "Come on, I want to show you my office and some photos of the pack." Curious, I follow him down a dirt track lined with spruce trees and stop in front of a rustic log cabin, an old Chevy pick-up parked in front. Wild columbines nestle by the rustic stairs leading to a large deck. He pulls me through the heavy cedar door, and I gasp as I see mounts of all kinds on the log walls. Bears, elk, cougars, and a few I don't recognize. He tells me to sit down and relax. I look around the large room and notice the details – caramel leather sofa, buffalo rug on the floor, large fireplace of moss-covered rock, and a live-edge pine coffee table. The room is surprisingly neat but smells of wet dog. Taylor returns with a Coke in one hand and several books – photo albums. He hands me the Coke and asks me what I think about the house. I tell him it is very warm and inviting, but it smells like wet dog.

He chuckles. "The pack members are sometimes allowed in here."

"Isn't it dangerous to have them in here?" I ask.

"Yes, at times." He then pulls up the sleeves of his shirt, exposing bite marks, scars, and a few deep depressions where flesh has been torn out of his forearm. "Annie, these wolves are still wild animals and can never really be trusted, but I do most of the time."

He opens one of the photo albums and shows me the wolves he has rescued over the years, names for all of them.

I hear the sadness in his voice as he talks, and I reach over to squeeze his shoulder. He jerks away from me. "No Annie, don't touch me. The pack will be frantic when they smell you on me."

"I'm sorry; I didn't know."

He sternly replies, "Remember, I am their alpha."

CHAPTER TWO

glance at my watch and tell Taylor I must go if I am to get through the pass before dark. He nods and asks me to please come again soon and that he'd like to visit more.

"I will, Taylor. I would like to learn more and perhaps we could go to dinner at Tova's in Twin Lakes." He winks at me and leads me to my car; I hear snarls from the fence line. In my car, I watch Taylor in my rear-view mirror as he removes his flannel shirt and goes over to the pack. His white t-shirt does not cover his muscular biceps and clings to his stomach. *Oh yes, Dr. Taylor, I will definitely visit again soon.*

I drive back to Aspen, anxious to get home and take a hot shower. The wet dog scent clings to my clothes and I am chilled from the open car window. It's been a nice day, but I'm ready to collapse on the bed. Once home and in the shower, my pine-scented body wash quickly removes the scent of the wolves, and I get dressed in purple sweats. I turn on the gas fireplace in the library and pull a book from the shelf: *Wolves, a Study of the Apex Predator*. The book stimulates my thoughts as I picture Taylor and six sets of golden eyes following him down a dirt path.

The first chapter explains the pack mentality and how each member can contribute and be submissive to the pack leader. An alpha, provider of food, the best hunter and protective of all family members. I learn some of the pack habits and realize why the interaction at Taylor's had so many snarls: Taylor

Katherine Zartman

is the alpha. I become uneasy when I read the breeding rights of the alpha, the only one permitted to breed with the strongest female. I learn the signs of body posture, anger, hunger, willingness to breed, and above all, submission to the alpha. Always below him, tails tucked under and ears flattened, skull pulled in to their thick, muscled shoulders. I chuckle when I think about how I've seen this behavior in humans.

There are many photos of wolves throughout the book and I learn that Taylor's wolves are Timberwolves; their territory extending from the mountainous U.S. to the northern Canadian providences, preferring the colder climates, as do their natural prey. Pack animals hunt as a coordinated group, wearing out their prey until it cannot continue its flight from the bared canines of the pack, led by the alpha and his chosen mate – another premier hunter. I look at my watch: 11:30 p.m. I reluctantly close the book and curl up beneath the down comforter on my bed. Dreams of silvery white fur, flannel shirts and golden eyes lead to a restless night. I wake early and venture to downtown Aspen. I visit my favorite bakery, drawn by the scent of sinful treats and clutching a bag from the bookstore. Several coffee table books and a primer on their behaviors. Tomorrow I will visit Taylor and show him how much I have learned about his pack mates. My real reason, of course, is to learn more about the alpha, the pack leader. I briefly allow myself the memory of his green eyes and his rugged, handsome face. Another memory follows of his perfectly pitched snarls at the fence line and produces goosebumps, along with a tremor of fear.

CHAPTER THREE

I call Taylor to make sure he will be home and not hunting, as I wish to visit tomorrow. He does not answer, and I listen to his soft voice announcing that he is with his wolves. "Please leave a message and I'll return the call. If this is an emergency, call my cell phone – but only if it is an emergency as the sound or the vibration of the phone disturbs the wolves." Further intrigue and a pull to the to the green eyes. I leave a brief message for the good doctor and a phone number so he can respond. I recognize the number when the phone rings and try to calm the nerves below my waist. My hand travels down over my abdomen and presses hard.

He soon returns my call. "Annie, hi, can't wait to see you. Pack a bag in case it gets too late for a trip back through the pass."

"Thanks, Taylor," I respond. "I'll see you mid-morning; plan to have lunch at Tova's." Tova is a good friend, Swedish, blonde, blue eyes, owner of the wonderful B&B and restaurant in Twin Lakes. I contemplate calling her in advance, then punch in her number.

"Tova, hi. I will be in town tomorrow with Dr. Taylor for lunch. Will you reserve the Aspen suite in case it is too dark to drive back?"

"Sure, Annie," she says. "I look forward to hearing about Dr. Taylor's wolves. See you tomorrow!"

I hang up the phone and wonder if I have been too

forward with Dr. Taylor. I felt a chemistry during our first talk and I'm sure he had felt the same. Was my scent of gardenias a draw to a predator? I somewhat dismiss the thought and spend an hour in a warm bath, removing any hair from my legs and being overzealous with the gardenia scented oil I use to soften my skin. Feeling more like an excited teenager, I scan the body facing me in the mirror. My forty-five years has taken a few hits here and there but overall, I am pleased with my reflection. The muscles around my middle are still tight, my breasts still maintain good lift – the inevitable downward droop still awaiting its chance to age me. I tweak each nipple and they respond to the pressure of my fingers. I pull on sweats and curl up with my new wolf books to learn more about the pack. I drift off to sleep, faint howls fading in the background.

I pack my soft, gray leather duffle bag and dress in a sexy black lace thong and matching bra, assuming Taylor will assert his power as he removes them. I drive a bit more recklessly over Independence, tires slipping close to the edge. I pass the summit and realize the altitude has hastened my breathing. Another half hour and many sharp, dangerous turns slow my rapid heartbeat as caution overtakes the building excitement. My Jeep is such a pleasure to drive and I smoothly turn into Taylor's rutted dirt drive.

Taylor is at the fence and motions me to stay in the car. The pack follows his movement to my car, and he greets me with a big smile. I tell him to pack a small bag of clean clothes; I don't want dinner with a wolf.

He grins and tells me to stay in the car. "I'll be ten minutes."

I relax in the leather seat and watch as the pack follows his movement to the house. Once the door closes, the eyes of the pack travel back to me and a few snarls echo over the fence.

Taylor has changed into tight, washed jeans and a blue,

long-sleeved shirt, soft brown ankle boots, and he's carrying a bulging backpack. I swear I hear him snarl a low, guttural sound as he opens the car door and sits down on the passenger side. He warns me not to touch him while in view of the pack. I nod and make a smooth turn to exit. Six heads follow the Jeep, ears raised. I hear a chorus of howls as I turn onto the highway.

"Annie, I was so pleased when you called me," Taylor says as he squeezes my knee, sending a tremor through me. He talks about Katana, the dominant female who will watch over the pack while Taylor is gone. I return his action and squeeze his knee, and I ask him if he realizes what I want. He nods and runs his hand up my thigh. "I want this, too, Annie."

I pull into Tova's B&B and Taylor puts his arm around my waist and bends to kiss my neck. His lips travel up and down it as he leans into me. "Tell me if I get out of line. I do have a few wolf instincts and I'm unaware when they are different than human ones."

I kiss Taylor on the cheek and tell him, "Just don't bite me." He smiles and we go inside. Tova leads us to a sunny table with a view of the Twin Lakes dam. Water is being released into the lakes as more snowmelt funnels into the reservoir. We order bison burgers served with warm German potato salad and Tova's hot bacon vinegar dressing. It is the best!

We finish lunch and decide to walk to the dam to see the torrents of water pouring into the lake. We have both taken the tour of the dam before, so we decline an invitation by a tour guide and wander across the observation deck, catching the fierce spray from the water pressure. Cold, clear Colorado water flows into the lakes, bringing nutrients to its inhabitants. We talk about Taylor's practice, his years of school and finishing his doctorate at the University of California, Davis, recognized as the best veterinary school in the U.S. I realize

Taylor is a very smart man, dedicated to all animals, his preference, wolves.

We walk back to Tova's, each of us with hands in the other's back pockets, feeling one another's backsides. Inside, we get coffee and Tova gives me the key to the Aspen suite. I take the key and once we get to the suite, a roaring fire greets us – a nice welcome as we are both a bit chilled from the spray at the dam. Taylor wraps his arms around me and nuzzles my neck again. We stand in front of the fire for several minutes as we kiss deeply. He pulls from me and tells me, "Bath time. I don't have a tub at my house, but I have always loved it."

I nod and we shift to the bathroom. The large free-standing tub slowly fills, and we are both somewhat shy as we take off our shirts. We are each naked from the waist up and hug tightly. My breasts teasing his chest hair, he whispers, "I want you, Annie," and I respond with a pull on his zipper. I inch down his jeans, pulling his underwear to follow. All shyness disappears and Taylor groans as he pulls my jeans off and I stand before him in my black thong. I bend and kneel before him, kissing his erection and pull his generous length deeper into my mouth. He groans again and pulls my head up, asking if he needs to use a condom. I smile and whisper, "No, you are good to go. I had a tubal years ago." I pull his hand and we sit down in the hot, fragrant water in the tub. He pulls me against his chest and twists my nipples, one hand drifting lower until I feel fingers inside me. He swirls his fingers and gently pulls my legs farther apart. He finds my clitoris and starts to tease it. I feel his erection pressing against my backside and he says, "Sit on me, Annie."

"No," I say. "I want you in bed but first I need to clean you; rid you of the wolf scent."

"Sorry. I don't even smell it."

I smile and grab the body wash, slowly circling it over his

chest, arm and neck. I reach down and swirl my hands around his erection, and he says, "Careful. You are going to unman me." I swiftly push down on his shoulders until his head disappears under the water. I release his shoulders and he pops up frantically, wiping his eyes. "Hey, what are you doing?" I laugh and pour shampoo in his hair. I scrape my fingers through his scalp, and he groans with satisfaction. "The pack would love this."

"Well, Taylor, none of your wolves are going to share my bath." I pull him down again and squeeze the suds from his hair, lean forward and smell only shampoo, no wet dog. I reach for a hand towel and rub his hair until it no longer drips in his eyes. We both stand and dry ourselves, his erection pressing against my backside. I remove the down pads from the center of the bed and lie down, opening my legs and waiting for Taylor to join me.

"God, Annie, I need this." He takes me too tentatively at first and I press his ass forward, encouraging him to go faster. I wrap my legs around his hips and pull him deeper into me. Our breathing is labored, and we are both sweating as we grind against each other. Taylor yells out that he can't hold it anymore and with a low snarl, he climaxes. He stills and brushes his face on my neck and under my chin. I rub his back, enjoying the feel of the muscles rippling beneath my fingertips. Taylor rolls off me, kisses my shoulder and says, "This is going to get serious, fast."

I press my breasts against him and whisper, "I think it already has, Taylor."

"No, Annie, the pack will have to accept you before I can." I frown and ask him why. He hesitates and then tells me, "The pack is my family; they are my kids. I love them and they love me. I am their leader, the alpha. I know this sounds strange to you, Annie, but the pack dominates my life. I'll show you next time you come to the practice."

My emotions war with me. Does this man think he is a wolf? "Taylor, I need to think on this. I want a man for a partner, not one who considers his wolf instincts more than me."

"Hush, Annie. Just trust me and you'll know what I mean. But right now, I want to show you how much of a man I am." He pulls me to him and squeezes my waist. Pulling my breast to his lips, he draws it into his mouth and sucks, then releases it and pulls its twin to his mouth. His hands travel down and capture my sex; he rubs and grunts and pulls back the covers. He stands and goes to the bathroom; I hear him urinate and return with a warm, soapy washcloth. He gently spreads my legs and begins to clean me after I nod my okay. He pulls the cloth over me and removes the traces of semen. Then, he bends, taking my clitoris in his mouth and pushes his fingers slowly into me. "I love this, Annie. You give to me and I give to you. Be patient with me. I'm not warped; you will understand when you see me with the pack." He continues with his fingers and then pushes his erection into me, slowly pulling in and out, in and out. I again curl my legs around his hips and feel my climax building. Taylor moans and once again releases.

CHAPTER FOUR

The sun wakes us, streaking through the European lace sheers. Taylor kisses me and tells me, "I want you again, and then I'll have to shower so I don't have your scent on me." We have gentle sex and then Taylor smacks my ass, heading to the bathroom. He carefully cleans himself, then lets me know not to hug him, but that we can hold hands. We head down to have a nice breakfast; Swedish crepes and sugared mountain blueberries, served on Tova's delicate pine-cone dishes, along with mugs of fragrant coffee. I am surprised when Taylor lifts the vase of fragrant yellow roses that Tova grows behind the B&B. He thanks Tova for her wonderful attention to detail and pays our bill.

Back at the clinic, Taylor tells me, "I have to neuter four horses and then I have a surgery on a bull that damaged its eye on barbed wire. I'll pick you up when I'm done, and we can go to my place." Three hours later, we get a chance to talk.

"So," I ask, "What is your first name? How old are you?"

"Well, my first name is actually Edward, but I never use it," Taylor begins. "To everyone around here, I'm known as Wolf Taylor, even down at the bank. And I'm forty-three; how old are you?"

"I'm forty-five," I say. "Older than you, but I suspect maybe not as wise."

We drive down to the practice and Taylor explains what he wants me to do. "Stay in the car and just watch. Don't get upset, blow your horn or yell. The pack will show signs of aggression because they know you are here, so I need to communicate to them that you are a friend, not an enemy."

I swallow the fear that is crowding my thoughts as Taylor squeezes my hand, then walks over to the fence. Rubbing his hands in the dirt, he swiftly climbs over the fence. The pack is on him, licking his jaw and rubbing their snouts under his chin. One of them, I think perhaps the large female he calls Katana, bends her front legs, drops her head and flattens her ears, he behind still in the air. I recognize this as submissive behavior. Taylor greets her with cheek rubs as another female wolf approaches. Katana turns and snarls at her rival, and the two males stand and watch. One starts to snarl, and Taylor responds with his own. The young male flattens and shows an attitude to Taylor that seems to say, "Okay, I give up." Giving Katana a final nuzzle to her cheek, Taylor stands, and the pack comes over and brushes against his legs, a transfer of scent.

I realize Taylor's position and how he has been accepted by the pack; how he has earned it and how they all have become a loving group – family that will fight or die for him. I begin to understand why the pack needs to accept me in order for Taylor to be with me. They must accept my scent on him and my status as his breeding female. So strange to consider this conversation between species. I grin as a thought flits across my mind, seeing Taylor morph into a wolf. Taylor again vaults over the fence and saunters over to the Jeep. He opens the door, presenting his back to the fence, and pulls me into a hug. He kisses me and settles into the seat. "Well, Annie, what do you think?"

"I think I understand the bond with the pack; however, how do you think they will accept me?"

He squeezes my hand. "I will come up with a plan. Slow, baby steps until I can get you over the fence in their territory. I will know when that happens and I will not let them harm you, but when that time comes, you must show them no fear. They can sense weakness and will attack when assured of winning."

I stare at him. "Taylor, you are scaring me!", but he assures me that I will earn the pack's trust and that he will keep me safe. He tells me that it will be a busy week for the practice but that he would like to come to my house on Thursday, and then both of us will see the pack on Friday.

"Now hug me, Annie. I just need a small scent of you on me and I'll walk by the pack." He leans over to kiss me, and I run my hands over his chest muscles as we say goodbye. He slowly walks over to the fence and down the gauntlet of snarls and raised ears. Yes, they know their leader has contacted an enemy.

I return to Aspen and spend the evening reading more about the mysterious wolf. I begin to accept the need for Taylor to bond with his four-legged family but as I stand on only two, I cannot be a dominant female. I remain in my clothes for a while, smelling of wet dog and a reminder of what is to come. I will never be a Jane Goodall, but perhaps I can learn to understand the animal kingdom and its language of scent.

Thank God Taylor doesn't rescue bears; a wolf has much more appeal than a grizzly. I go to the kitchen and fix a turkey sandwich for lunch, then follow it with a hot bath. Time to relax as a human for a while.

CHAPTER FIVE

I have cleaned and straightened the house, planned lunch and dinner and arranged spring flowers for fragrance and color. My condo is ready for Taylor to see and I am ready as well. Taylor arrives and after a short tour of the condo, he pulls me into a tight hug, his hands caressing as we share a hunger for one another.

He drops his hands and slowly unbuttons my blouse, eases it off my shoulders, and bends to kiss and suck my breasts. He rubs my neck and chest and his breathing soon becomes frantic. "Annie, Annie, I need you." We shuffle to the bedroom, hands and lips rediscovering each other and I force him to the mattress. I jerk his jeans and underwear off and squeeze his erection, drawing it to my mouth. Taylor is forceful in return and holds my head in place. I feel a sense of panic rising and just as I'm desperate to breathe, he releases my head and jerks my pants down. He is on top of me before I can adjust and with the panic now driving him, he loses himself and bites my neck. I am quiet for a few minutes, conflicting thoughts racing through my mind.

"Taylor," I whisper, "talk to me."

"Christ, Annie, give me a minute to calm down!" Stricken, he looks at me. "Did I hurt you?" He strokes my face and I see tears rolling down his cheeks.

"What is it, Taylor?" He pulls my hair back, exposing the bite and then he leans in, slowly licking the blood away. Fear and panic bring tears to my eyes and I can hardly breathe. *God, what is wrong with this man?*

As if he can read my thoughts, Taylor softly whispers, "I'm so sorry. Please, let me explain. I'm afraid, Annie, I'm afraid. I couldn't stop thinking about you driving here and I didn't sleep last night. I don't want to think about letting you go; the pack just has to accept you and I'm so worried that they won't. I don't know what to do. They were giving me dangerous signals when they caught your scent and I don't know how to get them to accept you." Tears continue to roll down his face and I can feel his pain and anguish. "Help me, Annie, help me!"

I wipe his tears and say, "Don't worry, we will figure this out. You know the pack and you can interpret their language."

He kisses me in return, whispering, "I'm fucked up. I'm dangerous, and unable to control myself around you. The alpha in me overcame the human and I bit your neck."

I take his face in my hands and say, "I kind of understand the conflict, Taylor, and I will trust you to get it under control. Now, settle down and make love to me; no biting allowed."

His faces relaxes and a smile threatens to emerge. "Annie, Annie," and he licks and kisses his way downward. I realize his intention and say, "No, Taylor, I'm dirty." He ignores me and buries his head in my sex. I writhe and wiggle beneath him and whisper for him to take me. He wipes his wet face on my breasts, moans loudly and climaxes inside me.

"Oh Annie, I need you and I love you."

I look at him. "Taylor, we are still strangers. Take this slow."

"No, Annie," he insists. I feel it. I feel it and my heart struggles not to explode when I'm with you." He pulls my hand over his runaway heartbeat and I replace it with my lips. Time for lunch!

Taylor wants a shower with me before lunch and we

stand under the hot water, desperately clutching each other. Suddenly overcome with emotion, Taylor sinks to the floor, pulling me with him, and sobs into my neck, "Annie, Annie, Annie."

I clutch him to me and gently rock him, his body shuddering through the crisis. *Deep, deep pain must cause this man to break down in front of a woman like this; aren't men supposed to be stronger than this? Openly crying and exposing your soul in front of a virtual stranger?* "Are you okay to stand, Taylor?"

He nods and I turn off the shower and wrap him in a towel. He is shivering so I wrap my arms around him and lead him to bed. He is desperate to get control over his emotions but unable to do so. Sobs continue and he voices his shame. "I don't know what is wrong with me. I just don't know."

"I don't know, either, Taylor, but I do know that you need to let it go." I hold him closer. Cry over the pain and sadness; I'm here – just let it go."

"Christ, Annie," as he starts to cry again, great, heaving sobs, his body quivering with emotion. It continues for several minutes and I place my hand over his frantic heart. He slowly calms, kisses me and says, "I'm sorry, I'm sorry."

"Hush," I say. "We will figure this out. Now, stop being a blubbering mess. I'm hungry and need a drink."

Taylor follows me to the kitchen and watches carefully as I put rum, ice and pineapple juice together into a pitcher. I forgo the lime slices and take a long draw from a glass. Taylor follows my lead and bends to smell the flowers on the counter. I smile, take his hand, and lead him to the library. We build a fire and sit next to each other, staring into the flames to soothe our raw emotions. We don't talk; just sip our drinks and look at each other. He leans his head on my shoulder and strokes his fingers back and forth over my hand. He closes his eyes, bringing my hand to his lips, and whispers, "I love you, Annie, I love you."

I don't respond as I stroke his cheek. Within minutes, I realize that he is asleep. I pull the fuzzy gray blanket from the back of the loveseat, cover us both and curl up on his legs. Warm and safe, I close my eyes and sleep comes.

Taylor shifts and I look up at him. He smiles and says, "Lunch? I'm hungry." I nod and we head back to the kitchen, where I make chicken salad sandwiches and heat up some of my homemade chicken soup. Taylor pours each of us a glass of iced tea, and we sit at the kitchen table and enjoy our lunch. He picks up my hand and brings it to his lips; I do the same with his.

We are silent until he draws me back to the library. "I want to try to explain. Please, Annie, just listen."

I nod and silently sit down, watching him.

He begins. "I have lived with this pack for ten years, and a smaller one for eight years before that. They are family to me, and I've acquired many of their instincts. I bit your neck because I was panicked at what I was feeling. I haven't been with a woman for years and I just didn't realize how much I have become like the pack. I scared you and I scared myself. I am sincerely sorry for what I did and for the break down over control of my emotions. I really had no idea I could openly cry and carry on the way I did. You encouraged me to let go and I finally did, much to my surprise. Now, I want you to honestly tell me how you feel and if we have a chance to fix this. I've bared my soul to you; please give me some of it back. I'm just too broken right now. Please, Annie, please."

I gently kiss him and say, "I'll try, though I don't speak wolf. Please, just listen, Taylor. I have never witnessed such powerful emotions and fear. I was honestly ready to bolt, but your stress held me to you. It was like a nightmare with my eyes open; I truly thought my heart was going to explode. But now that the immediate crisis is over and I can think about it, I've realized: you drove me to fall in love with you, too. I think it's the only way I can respond to what I witnessed. You have changed my life, Taylor, and now we need to decide how we can live with the new one."

"Oh, Annie," he sighs with relief, "Annie, I love you." He hugs me passionately and kisses me deeply.

I pull back from him, hold his head in my hands and tell him softly, "I love you, too, Taylor. Now come to bed. I want to feel you inside me."

He lays me gently on the bed and covers me with his warm body. He embraces me, my arms held against his flesh. I feel his erection against my thigh, and he releases my arms and slowly enters me. We make love silently, climaxing together.

"Thank you, Annie, thank you," he sighs. "I want to discuss tomorrow. I need to go back because I have to feed the pack and I want you with me, not beyond the fence but in front of it. I need to see their response to you along with the warnings to me. You're strong, Annie, you can do this. You will have to obey me without question or hesitation."

"Yes, Taylor," I say. "I think I can do that; I know you will protect me."

He grabs me and says, "I want to dirty you up again – you on top of me – and then a hot shower." I mount him and he clutches my backside, pulling me to him and rocking his hips. He rolls me over and says, "I want to get you off before I do," and he massages my clitoris, fingers stroking inside me.

I whisper, "I'm close; take me hard, Taylor."

He slams into me time after time. "Come with me, Annie, come," and we both shout through our release. We stay prostrate for several long moments until I feel him lift me to the shower. He is gentle and tender as he begins to soap and clean me. He massages my sex with the body wash, and I wince and pull back from him. He asks what's wrong and I tell him that I'm sore.

He turns the water off and carries me to the bed. He tells me to pull my knees up and spread them. I look at him. "What do you want to do, Taylor?"

He smiles. "I want to examine you. I am a doctor, you know."

I hesitate, then agree. "It's embarrassing, Taylor, but I trust you."

He leans down and I feel his fingers trace across my sex and gently part my vagina. "You are red and bruised down here; I've been too rough with you. Do you have any massage oil?" I nod and tell him it's in the bathroom vanity. He goes to the bathroom and returns with the oil and a hand towel. He sets the towel on the nightstand and heads to the kitchen to heat the oil in the microwave. He returns and slides the towel under my backside. Testing the temperature of the oil, he gently starts to massage me softly, rubbing it into my vagina as he pulls his other hand to my clitoris; circling, rubbing, and I moan. He laughs, "You're enjoying this, aren't you, Annie?"

"Yes, yes," I continue to moan, "please continue your exam, Dr. Taylor."

He brings me to a shattering climax and smiles. I look at him and say, "You are so naughty, Dr. Taylor. I may need to schedule regular visits with you."

He kisses me and gently cleans the excess oil from me. I reach over and pour some oil on my hands and begin to slide it up and down his erection. He tucks his hips up and groans with pleasure. My hand continues and I use my other hand to massage his balls and run up past his anus, through his buttocks and back down, all while continuing to stroke his erection. He wants me to speed up and I tell him, "No, just relax and feel it. Let your climax build." I continue with both hands and he moans loudly, ejaculating all over my hands.

"Dear God, Annie! That was so good, so good!"

"My pleasure, Dr. Taylor, my pleasure."

I bring a warm washcloth and clean us both. I hug and kiss him. "Sleep well, baby, sleep well." We spoon together, exhausted, and sleep through the night.

CHAPTER SIX

I wake early and let Taylor sleep a little longer. I brew some hot tea and make breakfast omelets: eggs, mushrooms, green onion, and cheese, and start some bacon. Taylor comes into the kitchen naked and I admire his body. He nuzzles my neck and I tell him to go put some clothes on because he's too distracting. We sit and have a leisurely breakfast, silent about the stress forthcoming in the day. Rain is sputtering at the window and I hope that it isn't an omen for the day.

We leave Aspen and drive back over the pass in Taylor's truck for the benefit of the pack. "Remember, Annie," he says sternly, "do exactly as I tell you."

When we arrive, we step out of the truck. He puts his arm around me and greets the pack. Snarls and ears upright. He answers with his own snarl and the two males back up from the fence. "Annie, go to the cooler and bring me back six pieces of meat."

I do as I'm told. He touches each piece and hands them to me, instructing me to throw the meat over the fence, one piece at a time. He cautions me to not extend my arm over the fence, answering the snarls and growls from the pack with his own. He carefully watches everything and again circles his arm around my waist. Katana, the big female, is the first to return to the fence. I raise my hand to pull my hair back and Taylor snaps at me, "Put your hand down, Annie, and don't raise either of them!" He snarls again as the other females join

Katana at the fence. She flattens her ears and pulls her head to her chest. Taylor gasps and softly says, "Katana, Katana, of course you understand. Annie, I need you to be brave and do what I ask."

I swallow, my heart slamming in my chest, as Taylor instructs, "Go over to the fence where Katana is, keep your hands down and reach over slowly to rub her snout, not the top of it. Do you understand? Nod if you do; this is critical."

I slowly nod and move to get close to the fence as golden eyes watch me, snarls from all except Katana. She stares at me as I hear Taylor say, "Slowly bring your hand to her chest, under the snout. Do not go any higher and make sure to maintain eye contact with her."

I slowly ease my hand through the fence and up her chest, feeling the rough fur and staring into golden eyes. It is unnerving, but I do it. Taylor lets out a sigh and tells me to back away from the fence, never losing eye contact. I back away as Taylor leaps over the fence. Katana crawls over to him and I shout to Taylor, "Watch – the male is showing aggression!" He looks over at the male and nods. The male rushes over to Taylor and bares his teeth. Taylor is paralyzed for a split second, then lays down in the dirt, extending his arms in front of him, his behind in the air. I gasp as I recognize Taylor's act of submission.

The male moves to Katana and she flattens her ears, presenting her backside to him. Taylor crawls to the fence and is over it in a flash. He pulls my hand and leads me to the truck, pushing me to the seat as he follows me in. He hugs me tightly. "Annie, that was the hardest thing I have ever done, and I struggled to make the decision. You were perfect and made it possible."

I kiss him and whisper, "I know you gave up your status as the alpha; now you are mine, not theirs."

"Yes, Annie," he agrees, "yours, not theirs."

Tears and tension break loose from both of us, and we rock quietly together until Taylor shifts and starts the truck. We drive down to the house as he is kissing me and he says, "I need a drink. Do you want one?"

"Yes, I could use one."

"Bourbon and seven?" Taylor asks, and I nod. He turns to me with the drinks and says, "Let's go to Tova's; it's too late for the pass. I'm going to pack a bag for us. Sweats okay for you?"

I ask about just staying at his house and Taylor shakes his head. "I don't have a good shower except at the office and there are too many reminders here."

I understand, so I pull my phone and let Tova know that we are coming. Once we get there, she has lasagna, hot rolls and a bottle of red wine ready for us. The meal and the wine disappear quickly. Once again in the Aspen suite, we are greeted with a glowing fire in the fireplace and more fragrant, yellow roses, along with two fluffy, white robes on the warming rack. "Let's shower," Taylor suggests, frowning as he says it. "I know I smell like the pack."

We hug and kiss, stepping into the shower to remove the wet dog smell. We wrap ourselves in the warm robes and sit on the loveseat, the fire a boon to our souls. "You were amazing today, Annie. It could have been much worse for both of us."

I shyly smile and say, "Now I have power over you and not the pack. How do you think they will be with you now, Taylor?"

Sighing in thought, he says, "I have no idea, but I know I can't go beyond the fence anymore. I'm not a pack member anymore; I am exiled from it. Now hush, I want to make love to you. How are you down there? Should I do another exam?"

I laugh and say, "No, I'm fine. Just make love to me, we need it."

He pulls open the sash on my robe and caresses my breasts. I turn to him and open his robe, bending to his erection. He allows me a few moments to suck on him and then tugs me to the bed. "I need to make love to you, Annie. Tell me if you are sore and I'll stop."

"I will, Taylor," I assure him. "Just be gentle."

He slowly pushes into me, setting a slow pace. He asks if it's okay for him to continue and I nod. Easing in and out, in and out, he notes that I am dry. "I need something to lubricate you. I have my vet bag; let me check for something." He searches and smiles as he holds up Vaseline. "Don't worry, it's sterile. I always use a sterile scoop to get it on my gloves." He pulls a gob out on his fingers and spreads my legs, putting his fingers in me and stroking my clitoris. He rubs back and forth. "Better baby, much better."

"Make me come this way, baby; it feels so good," I pant as I erupt on him. Turning to him as I place him inside me, "That was so nice, Taylor. You are so sweet, so gentle. I love you."

"I love you, too, Annie. So much." We both start to cry, and I place my head on his chest while he strokes my back and I fall asleep on him.

CHAPTER SEVEN

I wake when he shifts during the night and pull him to my front, his butt tight to my groin and my arm around his belly as morning dawns. "Good morning," I say as he wakes. "Can we spend the day here?"

"Sure," Taylor says. "The pack has been fed and I don't take vet appointments on the weekends. Can you handle my sweats and share a toothbrush?"

I smile and nod, saying, "Yes, but hustle up. Breakfast." We go downstairs for bacon and eggs, toast, and melon. Tova will run laundry for us and we decide to walk the lake. We talk about the pack, Taylor's voice thick with emotion as he talks about how difficult it will be for him to not interact with the pack. He grows silent and whispers, "Don't let me get moody; keep me happy," and I promise to do so. We walk the shoreline and several fishermen greet us, asking how the pack is. Taylor lets them know the pack is fine and introduces me as his girlfriend.

Continuing our walk, I point out that everyone seems to know him. He nods and explains that he is the only vet for the Department of Wildlife as well as the only large animal vet for the entire area. "Oh, Taylor, I had no idea; I'm so proud of you!"

He grins and hugs me, and we decide to drive over to Buena Vista and do a little shopping. Sweats, underwear, toothbrushes, and a few other personal items. I pay the bill and Taylor asks why I seem to be so free with money. I let him know that I have a lot of family money, a large bank account and that I own three houses in Aspen. He laughs and jokes, "Well, Annie, now I love you even more. I never thought I could have a rich girlfriend!"

After a few minutes, he turns to me. "Annie, it just doesn't feel right to me to call you my girlfriend. You are so much more to me, but I don't know where this can go."

"Baby," I say, "I don't know, either, but I think I want to grow old with you and share everything I have."

Taylor smiles. "God, Annie, I love you and I would marry you today if you said yes. I have only had two other relationships before you, both short and casual, given my lifestyle and my canine family. You are the only one I have every loved and felt comfortable with. I've bared my soul to you and I would die for you."

I kiss Taylor deeply and place my hands over his rapidly beating heart. "You have my heart and soul, too, Taylor." We are quiet driving back to Twin Lakes, squeezing each other's hands. I consider our future and I'm amazed how quickly we have come to face it. "Taylor, why do you think you fell in love with me, and why do you want to marry me?"

He smiles and responds, "You are beautiful, honest, great in bed, and most of all, you understand me. You understand my soul. You've watched me fall apart in front of you. You are perfect for me. Your turn, why do you love me?"

"Taylor, you are the most interesting man I've ever met. You are handsome, successful, smart, and you allowed me to share the baring of your soul – a life changing moment for me. Not to mention, you gave me the best ever examination by a doctor, among other bedroom skills."

He laughs and says, "Well, in that case, I think it's time for a follow-up visit with Dr. Taylor. May I ask: when is your period due, Annie?"

A natural question from a doctor, I suppose, so I tell him not to worry. After an early entry into puberty, I had an early entry into menopause as well. I don't take hormones at all, and I let him know that it's probably why I am dry sometimes. It strikes me that I can discuss literally anything with this man.

We go directly to our suite back at Tova's and take a hot bath. Facing each other in the tub, I grab Taylor's foot and massage the instep, heel and pads. My fingers circle with intense pressure and clearly enjoying the pleasure, he brings his opposite foot to me so I can continue. The suds are evaporating so I drain the tub and Taylor swats my backside. "Come, Annie, I want to do that follow-up exam before dinner."

I laugh and go to the shopping bag, producing a bottle of strawberry-flavored massage oil. "Dr. Taylor," I say as he grins, "it's time to be naughty again."

I lay down, pull my knees up and spread them. Taylor puts a towel under me and spreads my knees wide, squirting oil on me. "Just relax, Miss Jacobs, and let me see how you are doing." He plunges fingers into me, swirling around and massaging the front wall of my vagina. He continues for several minutes and then brings his other hand to my clitoris as I wiggle and raise my hips in pleasure. He pulls my knees wider and dips his head. "Strawberry, mmm, good." I instruct him to put his fingers back in me as I am close, and he complies. I climax loudly, immediately wanting more. I drag his erection several times over my sex and guide him into me.

"Hot and heavy, baby, hot and heavy," he pants. "I want you so bad, Annie! Oh, God, I love you. I'm going to explode in you!"

We nap for a few hours, then go down to the restaurant for dinner. I see Tova and mention that we could use some clean towels and make arrangements for us to stay until Monday. After dinner, Tova asks Wolf if he can take a look at one of her female sheep as she is ready to lamb and seems to be in distress.

"Of course, Tova," Taylor says. "Let me just grab my bag and I'll take a look."

We go out the back door and hear the sheep before we even see her, her loud bleats a signal of pain to any ear. Taylor approaches her and goes down on one knee to probe her belly. He stands and pulls on a long blue glove so that he can insert his hand into the sheep's backside. "Tova, she is in active labor, but the lamb is not in position and she is hemorrhaging. I'll try to get the baby in birth position, but I think it is already dead. Annie, please try to soothe the mom, and Tova, if you would please, pull up her back leg and press down on the other one."

Tova does, and Taylor, sweating and grunting in the effort, tries to turn the lamb. The mother is still hemorrhaging, and the baby is very possibly dead. Tova says, "God's will. Can you save the mama?"

"I'll do my best for her," Taylor promises, "but first I need to deliver the baby." Again, he shifts and reinserts his gloved arm. "The baby is definitely dead; there's no heartbeat. And I'm afraid I'll lose the mama if I can't get it out." He pulls and pulls on the baby's legs but can't get it to the point of exit. "Annie, do you think you can help me?"

"Of course." I go over to him. "Tell me what you need."

"Well," Taylor starts, "I need to pull the head and shoulders down further because they are stuck on a pelvic bone. Then you could pull on the legs at the same time. Otherwise, I'm out of options here."

I look at Taylor, then at Tova, and say, "I'll try."

Taylor instructs me to put on a blue glove and to brace myself so that I don't fall if the baby comes out. I take a deep breath and steady my stance.

"This will happen fast if it works, Annie, so be ready. Put your hand in alongside mine until you feel the legs. Grab both of them above the knee and pull your hardest when I tell you; do not hesitate." He pushes his arm in further and I feel his muscles flex against my arm. A strong tug from him, then he yells, "Pull, Annie, pull!"

I pull with all my strength, the mother screaming, and I sense the baby sliding out. I back away, observing the bloody body of the baby still gripped in my hands. Taylor takes the body from me and kneels to check the mom. He pulls on fresh gloves as blood still pours from the sheep. He listens to her heart and shakes his head. He stands and tells Tova to say goodbye. "I can't save her. In the office, maybe, but not here."

Tova begins to cry and murmurs something in Swedish to the mama sheep. Taylor tells Tova that he will put the sheep to sleep so that she doesn't suffer and Tova nods. Pulling a syringe and vial from his pack, Taylor prepares the needle, then quickly injects it. Putting the needle in a bio bag, he asks Tova if she is in a residential burial zone.

"Yes," she nods, "I have had to do this before. John will take care of it." She bursts into fresh tears as Taylor hugs her, his eyes imploring me to take Tova away.

Tears roll down my cheeks and Taylor says, "Life and death, Annie. Life and death."

I follow Tova into the kitchen and she hands me antibacterial soap for my hands. "Do it twice for thirty seconds."

I do as she instructs while she opens a bottle of red wine, pouring each of us a glass. "Come, Annie. We go to dining room."

We sit at a window table, talking softly about the loss and how much she likes Taylor. "He is such a good man; you are so lucky, Annie." I tell her that I love him dearly and that we may marry soon, and she pats my hand. "He is the best and I know he will take care of you. A warm body to sleep against you. I envy you, Annie. Now, I must go and check orders. Let me know if I can make anything for you."

I tell her that I will, but it is after eight when Taylor comes in. He looks exhausted, and we head up to our suite for a shower. He takes a bottle of antibacterial soap out of his kit and says that he must use it after a death or surgery. He also pulls a garbage bag and dumps his clothes into it. I move to hug him, but he shakes his head no. He gets into the shower with the soap, and I watch as he scrubs himself and washes his hair. He rinses off and beckons me to join him. "Now you can wash me with the regular soap and hug me."

As I step into the shower and begin to clean him, he turns to me. "Christ, Annie. I'm sorry you had to witness that, and that I couldn't save them. I knew as soon as I examined the mama that the baby was dead, and that the mama was bleeding to death. I knew I would lose both of them, but I still had to try for Tova. Now you know where some of my pain and emotion come from. It's a direct part of me and I'm so glad you seem to accept and understand."

I grab his hand. "Oh, Taylor, I do understand, and it makes me love you even more. Are you hungry?"

He shakes his head, telling me he can't eat, and I feel the same. I call Tova, telling her not to worry about dinner and that maybe we will have coffee later. Taylor is on the bed, naked, eyes closed. I take a moment to admire his body, then move to the bed and kiss him. He asks if we can be celibate tonight as he is so tired, and I kiss him again. "Sure, just move over so I can spoon with you like last night."

He kisses me and shifts over. I cover him and pull on new sweats, no underwear, and socks. I make my way downstairs and a kitchen aide makes me some hot coffee. I return to the suite library and pull a book on wolves. I spend two hours learning how the alpha will now be a mortal enemy to the pack, killed if the opportunity presents itself. Chilled, I turn the lights off and snuggle up to Taylor. I kiss his white ass and pull it to my groin. Taylor shifts and draws me to him. "Can I?"

He is pressing his erection to me and I don't answer his question with words, only my body. I welcome him and we slowly speak a language known only to us.

The next morning, Tova presents us with apple streusel pancakes and then we check out. She refuses my AmEx card, looking to Taylor. "Paid in full, Wolf," she says. "You made it easier for me yesterday."

CHAPTER EIGHT

I hug Tova goodbye and we drive the fifteen minutes to the rescue. We stop at the fence line and Taylor is immediately alarmed. "What the fuck is going on?"

Every wolf in the pack is laying on the ground, the young male with its legs in the air, dead. Taylor sees this and exclaims, "God, Annie, the pack is sick!" He walks straight to the fence and snarls. A few wolves raise their heads in response and lay back down immediately. He instructs me to stay in the truck as he gets his dart gun.

"What?" I ask, alarmed. "Tell me."

"The pack is sick, and I won't be able to get blood tests unless they are down. Fuck. This is serious, I'm afraid." He walks up to the surgery suite in the office, unlocks the door, and soon returns with vials and syringes, and wearing a hazard suit, booties and blue gloves.

Again, he tells me, "Stay in the truck, Annie, but yell if you see any of the wolves rise to stand." He takes a posture at the fence and shoots three of the females with the tranquilizer darts. They yelp and try to get up but fall back down. Taylor can't reach the other female and the new alpha, so he turns to me.

"Watch them; I need to go over the fence to reach them." He vaults over the fence and darts Katana, along with the male who snarls and yelps when he feels the sting of the dart. He exits quickly and tells me that he needs to wait to make sure they are all truly down. He gathers the needles he needs to draw blood and pulls a revolver from a pocket and checks for ammo. Taylor tells me that he suspects the wolves must have some sort of dangerous virus and if so, that he will have to kill them.

He pulls his phone and makes a call. He listens and turns to me, tears streaking his face. "I called a hunter I know, and he told me there is a deadly virus running through the state affecting all kinds of animals. If they pack has it, they must be shot. I asked him to come over in case they need to be killed, so he will be here in about thirty minutes."

He looks over at the pack, none of the wolves moving, and goes over to the pack, again drawing blood from the three females and telling me to watch for movement. With the samples collected, Taylor says to me, "I need to look at this under the microscope; I won't be long."

He goes to the back building and prepares three glass slides with smears from the females. He notices right away the unusual appearance and dark spots in the smears. He has no idea what it is, but assumes the pack has the virus. They have to be killed. His family must die.

Taylor comes back to me, telling me what he's found – that the pack has some kind of a virus he doesn't recognize, but that Joseph, his hunter friend, said it is deadly and that the pack will have to die to protect other animals. Many rabbits, squirrels, and others come into their territory. If they were to pick up the virus, then be eaten by a predator, the virus would spread quickly.

Joseph arrives and talks softly with Taylor. Taylor nods to me, reminding me to watch for movement. Joseph pulls a shotgun from his truck and joins Taylor over the fence. I watch as Joseph walks over to the alpha first and places the shotgun to the back of the wolf's head, pulling the trigger. I see a spray of blood as the men turn to Katana. Taylor reaches out to pet her, but Joseph pulls him back to not touch her. He quickly cocks the shotgun and pulls the trigger, sending another spray of blood into the air. They walk over to the other dead male and shoot him, too, followed quickly by the three remaining females.

When it's over, Joseph puts down his shotgun and draws his phone from his pocket to make a call. Taylor looks at me, pain in his face and tears in his eyes. "We have to get the Department of Wildlife to come burn the bodies and bury them. Thank God I don't have to do it." Waiting for Wildlife to arrive, Taylor and Joseph drag the bodies together and talk softly.

Wildlife arrives very quickly with a large trailer attached to a truck. They pull on biohazard suits and tell Taylor, "So sorry, Wolf, but it had to be done." "This one is really dangerous." "Glad you called; we can't burn here – too much vegetation." They pull the trailer close to the fence and start throwing the wolf bodies into it. Joseph says he will follow them and then use their detox house before going home. Taylor thanks them but tells them he cannot go any further.

"No problem" the Wildlife guys say. "We will come back and detox the area for you. Wolf, give us your clothes and we will dispose of them." Taylor looks over at me, throws his revolver down to the dirt, then strips naked in front of all of us, including socks and shoes. He waves to the group, the guys grinning as they slowly drive out to the highway. Turning to me, he tells me to stay in the truck; that he needs a shower and clean clothes before he can touch me. I nod and watch as he picks up the revolver and walks to the surgery shower, his white ass building excitement in me as I watch.

Taylor showers and comes out ten minutes later with wet hair, sterile covers over his shoes. Strange, but he must keep a wardrobe in the suite. He walks over to the truck and slides into my arms.

I hold him and say, "I'm so sorry, Taylor. To lose your family all in one day, and with a bullet to the brain." He looks at me with tears running down his face. I pull him to my chest, and he heaves with loud emotion. "I'm right here. Just let go, baby. Weep for your loss, weep for your family." He squeezes me almost to the point of pain as his body continues to shake and shake. His grief visible throughout his body. I pull him over to sit on my lap and rock him back and forth, back and forth.

"God, Annie," he cries. "I can't stand this."

"Yes, you can, baby. You've lost your family, but you still have me," I say, holding him closer.

He shudders again and tears wet my shoulder. He wipes his nose on my shirt and shifts his weight to pull away from me, but I stop him. "No, baby, you aren't done yet. Just let me hold you."

Taylor relaxes a fraction and I kiss him, stroking his back. The frailty of such a strong man. It's like I hear his pain, without even a voice. I don't know how long we stay like this, but when he shifts again, I welcome his weight off my legs.

I look at him." I understand it this time, Taylor. I feel what your pain does to you and why. How it strips you of all your defenses, leaving you without a weapon to fight. I love you so much, Taylor. So much. You are my alpha, my master, and I submit to all your desires and needs."

"Oh, baby," he sighs. "Oh, baby, I love you and cherish you. You see inside me."

I kiss him. "Okay, enough for today. We need to get to Aspen before dark. I'll drive and you rest."

"I need you. And a hot bath," he says as he kisses me back. He scoots over to me and puts his head in my lap. I pull the lever to raise the steering wheel and tell Taylor to be good. He laughs and says, "Don't worry; I don't want you to be distracted."

CHAPTER NINE

I drive cautiously through the sharp curves along the narrow road, smiling when I see the sign for Maroon Bells: halfway home. I look down, thinking Taylor is asleep, his face tight against my sex. The road is wider in this section, so, feeling more secure, I run my fingers through Taylor's hair. I glimpse a few gray hairs and turn my attention back to the road, smiling to myself. *My sensitive, loving old man*.

Suddenly, I brake hard, waking Taylor as two large elk break from the trees right in front of the truck. It is dusk; their time to cross the road and make their way to the river for a drink. Taylor looks at me. "Quick reflexes, Annie."

I smile. "Thanks. We are almost home, and I'm starving. How about you?"

He nods, saying, "Let's just order a pizza. I haven't had one in years."

I hand him my phone, telling him to call Eddie's so we can pick it up on way home. Taylor laughs. "Home. Yes, we need to talk about home, but not today, baby. Not today."

"We have lots of time to decide our future," I agree. "Order a large supreme and a couple bottles of Coke. If we're going to be unhealthy, we should enjoy it. We can eat it in a hot bath."

Taylor calls and places our order, and fifteen minutes later we pull into the parking lot and collect our pizza, along with Eddie's good wishes. Taylor raises the box lid. "Smells wonderful. You know, I could get fat in Aspen."

"No, Taylor, I won't let you." I give him a sly look. "I love seeing your tight, muscular body and your smooth, white ass."

He laughs as we arrive, and we take the stairs up to my condo. Inside, I turn on the lights and Taylor starts our bath. I drag two of the dining room chairs to the bathroom to use as tables and grab a roll of paper towels. I turn on a classical CD, volume low, and Taylor comes up behind me, nuzzling my neck. I turn around and roughly tear his clothes from his body, and he does the same to me. Fully naked, we hug each other, and we kiss deeply; Taylor's mouth searching for answers, and his erection searching for solace. We remain tight together for several minutes before he smacks my ass and declares, "Come on, pizza's getting cold."

We hold hands and help each other into the tub. We grab slices of pizza and savor the treat, Eddie's marinara sauce clinging to our chins. Good thing we ordered a large as the pizza disappears quickly, the cold Cokes a perfect partner. Taylor leans toward me and licks sauce from my face, his tongue travelling down my neck in a quest for a nipple. He sucks and pulls, alternating between each nipple, as his fingers search underneath the suds for another body part. He is breathing hard and I pull his erection to me, bending to envelope it with my mouth. Eight inches of man strength quivers with need and Taylor guides me over it, firmly pulling my hips down to encompass all of him.

He lifts and pushes his hips to me and explodes with a violent shudder. "Sorry, Annie. I couldn't hold it."

I kiss him and we get out of the tub, wanting to feel each other and lengthen out against each other. Our need is a fire we cannot control. Taylor's erection presses against me as he slithers down my body, urging my legs apart. He buries his mouth on me and inserts fingers. I wiggle beneath him and we grind against each other, seeking release. We have stripped our resources, desperate to fill up again.

We both lay silent, hands over our beating hearts, when Taylor breaks the spell and asks if we can talk. I press my finger to his lips. "Not yet. We need more time, Taylor."

"Do you still love me, Annie?", panic rising as he asks.

"Hey," I assure him, "I love you more than life. I just think we can't talk about the future until we can forget the horror of today."

"Annie, Annie. I will never get over today," Taylor insists as he starts to cry, his body changing from calm to panic at lightning speed.

"Okay, Taylor, I see your need to release, so let it go."

He sobs, tears flowing, and I know he is fighting to hold his emotion in check, so I encourage him. "Show me, baby, show me. I need to see it. I can't kiss it away."

Before I know it, Taylor is biting me. Again and again, only stopping when I bite his shoulder, hard. He begs, "Again, Annie. Punish me. Bite me."

I bite him again, harder this time, and I taste blood.

"Again, Annie! Again!" Taylor shouts. Exposing his neck, I bite it, again drawing blood. His whole body bucks against me, tears falling as he pushes me away. "Enough. No more! Stop before I hurt you." I stop and kiss him, pulling his head to my chest and letting his tears run down my sternum. I gradually feel him calming down, and he strokes my neck. He runs his fingers over my bite marks and starts to tell me something, but I stop him.

"Shh. I know, I know. Stop punishing yourself. You didn't hurt me; you held back. I love you, Taylor, and I bite even harder than you did." He smiles as I kiss his tears away and lick the blood from his neck. I look into his eyes and ask, "So who won this one?"

"Oh, no contest," Taylor says. "You did, Annie."

Would anyone understand what happened? Could anyone really comprehend the screams of two desperate people, allowing ancient animal instincts to take control over us? We make love to each other again. Silent, our need not requiring voice. We sleep curled up against each other, searching for answers even as we slumber. The "why" I can understand, but the "what" still remains a mystery.

The next morning, Taylor shifts in bed and I nudge him, telling him to get up and dress. We need to talk, but not in bed. He kisses me and asks for coffee, so I pour two cups and draw him to the sofa in the library. I shield my bite marks with a sweater and Taylor turns on the gas to light a fire. He joins me on the sofa, and I cover us both with a blanket. We are awkward, neither of us willing to speak first.

I finally take a sip of my coffee and begin. "Brutally honest, Taylor, we survived. We are not hurt, we are human, and we love each other. We don't have to talk of this again, but I just want to assure you of the future."

He nods and I continue. "I am going to put the condo and my other two houses up for sale, and I want you to put your cabin up for sale as well." Taylor starts to say something, but I hold up my hand to silence him. "Just let me talk, baby. I need to get this out and you need to listen. We are both going to leave our old lives and start a new one, together. I will ask Tova if she knows of any properties in Twin Lakes, one large enough for a house, land, and ample space for your practice, but not for the rescue." Taylor looks at me, and I keep going. "Right now, you and I are the ones who need rescue. You can teach me to be a great assistant to you in your practice, and finally..." I pause, taking a deep breath. "I want you to marry me, grow old with me, and know that I will always love and cherish you. Take a minute, and then give me the right answer."

Taylor looks at me in amazement, never dropping his eyes. Taking my hand, he kisses me hard and says, "Annie, you know you already have my answer. Now, do we have any ice cream? I have a sweet tooth."

I laugh and whisper, "Chocolate."

Our new life begins, so along with the ice cream, I bring Taylor a pad of paper and a pen, telling him to write down what he would need to start a new practice. He hugs me tightly and starts his list, showing me the first item: "You by my side."

I pull the pad away from him and let him know that I have a need that's just a little more important right now. Taylor picks me up and gently carries me to our bed. We twist and pull, pushing, pounding, pressing – killing the demons and asking for a pardon. We explode together, all energy gone, and I pull blankets over us.

CHAPTER TEN

orning arrives and Taylor is not beside me; he's in the library, adding to his list. He has made some coffee and says, "I'm pretty good in the kitchen; eggs and toast?" I take a look at his list:

1. You by my side
2. Big closets, big tub, tiny puppy
3. Great garden, lots of flowers
4. Windows, curtains so we can walk around naked
5. More later

I laugh and he goes to the kitchen to make breakfast. Such a gentle man; my heart turns over with love for him. We have breakfast and then Taylor says that he needs to check his email, and I have things to do as well. I gather laundry, change the sheets and call my lawyer. We talk briefly, his reaction a surprise. I make a second call to my realtor and tell her to sell the condo and the other two houses. I also ask her to give me an estimate on Taylor's place.

"Wow," she says, "big changes, Annie, big changes. I'll be in touch."

I return to Taylor and ask him about his schedule. He has a few spays and neuters, a complicated birth surgery, and vaccinations; a pretty light schedule. He mentions that most of his emails are from clients sending kind words about the loss of his pack. "How about you, Annie?"

"Well," I ask, "how sure are you about marrying me?"

"More sure than anything else in life. I love you so much."

"You'd better because we are getting married in the next two weeks. I've also put the condo and my houses up for sale, and my realtor will get us an estimate on your place."

Taylor looks at me. "This is so fast, Annie. Are you sure?"

"Yes, I am," I say confidently. "We need to move ahead before the past interrupts our future. Hey, do you think I can go with you to your appointments?"

"Sure, Annie. You are a part of me now."

We also talk about the wedding. Taylor goes for the traditional: tux, white dress, lots of guests and food, but I suggest we go casual with white shirts, pressed jeans and a three-day honeymoon at Tova's. Taylor likes that idea and then asks, "Will you go with me to choose your ring? I have no idea where to begin."

"Just a simple band, no diamonds, is enough for me," I tell him. "Maybe a simple message of your love engraved on the inside. I also need to let you know that I spoke with my lawyer about making a new will and share everything I have with you."

Taylor shakes his head. "I don't deserve you, Annie."

I take him by the arm and guide him to our bed. "Taylor, you deserve everything I can give you and right now, I want to get something from you." We undress each other and I tell him to take me from behind, holding my breasts for support. I bend over, he holds my breasts, releasing them to guide his erection, and then slams into me. Drawing out slowly and then slamming into me again, he repeats the pattern, building to release.

"Jesus Christ, Annie, I never want to pull out of you, but I will because you need me. And you need to release as well."

I open the top drawer and he understands, grabbing the oil to squirt on me. He bends and manipulates my clitoris, sliding his hand back and spreading the oil. He slips his fingers in me, reading my body while he rotates his fingers and massages me. I am frantically raising my hips, searching for more. A powerful pressure explodes, and I pull back, too sensitive to have him in or on me.

"That was a good one, huh, Annie?" Taylor smiles. "You like my fingers in you."

"Loved it, Dr. Taylor," I smile back. "You are too good at reading signals."

He smiles and kisses me, and we head into the shower, where we massage each other with body wash and dry with my fluffy white towels.

I pull spaghetti sauce from the freezer, start the oven for garlic bread, and heat up a pot of water for noodles. Taylor comes into the kitchen, his towel still wrapped around his waist, asking what he can do to help. I tell him to open a bottle of cabernet or merlot; he opens the wine fridge as I shake my head. "Red wine I don't chill; it's in the library. I need to educate you a bit."

He winks and I swat his ass with the dish towel I am holding. He laughs and says, "Back in a minute."

The sauce is hot, noodles drained, and I hand Taylor plates and silverware for the dining table. We get everything to the table and sit down, clinking our wine glasses together in a silent toast. Taylor smiles at me. "Fancy, Annie, fancy."

"Spaghetti?" I wink. "Well, you know I like a bit of elegance in life."

"Tux, white dress, diamonds?" Taylor arches an eyebrow.

"No, Taylor, you know me. I need simple and down home even more."

After dinner, he kisses me as he stands to collect our plates. He rinses them and loads everything into the dishwasher, still just wearing his towel. I walk up behind him and pull the towel from his waist. "Dinner is over; you don't need an apron anymore."

I grab his ass and spin him to me, his erection already rising before my mouth is on him. He holds my head, guiding it back and forth. "Christ, Annie, you are too good at this." I know he is close, but I resist his attempts to pull me off him. "God, Annie, I can't hold it!" He shudders through his climax and sinks to his knees. I curl up on the floor next to him, playing with his hair and enjoying the warmth of the dishwasher door against me.

"You know, Annie, you are the only one to do that to me," Taylor points out. "In fact, the only one to ever have a mouth on me; I had no idea. There is one thing I have never done and always wanted to…" He blushes, holds my chin, and softly asks to put it in my ass. "I know it's supposed to feel much tighter and I want to try it."

"Just warn me," I say, "so I can be ready for you."

He laughs, tells me that he loves me, and we shift to the library. Taylor suggests that we watch a movie, so I tell him to go ahead and choose one. He looks over the packed shelves and pulls out Gladiator, one of my favorites. I put the movie in and adjust the TV input, then bring a pair of sweats to Taylor; too distracting when he's naked. We watch the film and make out a little, missing some of the good parts. The movie ends and Taylor lifts me and carries me to bed. No sex, just kisses, and we spoon together, exchanging body heat. We sleep well, content and happy.

I make French toast for breakfast and Taylor checks his emails as I wander through the condo, considering what I want to keep and what to donate. My realtor calls to let me know she already has a client who wants to see the condo, so I ask her to give me an hour and I'll leave the key under the mat. We straighten up, freshen the bathroom and Taylor vacuums the library rug. He tries to artfully drape a throw over the sofa, but I take it from him, shake it and softly drape it over the arm. I make sure the lights are all on, a fire is going, and I pull a few dead blooms from various flower arrangements throughout the condo. Good enough, we walk to town.

Taylor asks me if I think the condo will sell quickly, and I nod. "It should. I've put over $500,000 into improvements and updates, and the HOA fees are only $800 a month, low for Aspen. My realtor thinks I could get between two and three million for it."

Taylor whistles. "Wow, I had no idea. And that's not even counting your other two homes here. God, Annie, are you sure you want to share so much with me?"

I kiss him. "You will share everything I have. I'm living a dream with you." I put my arm around his waist, and we head into my favorite bakery. We order lattes, sourdough bread and fresh blueberry pastries, hot from the oven. Sitting at an outdoor table, we watch the parade of strange visitors that Aspen draws. Pink and blue hair, black hair and lips, Armani, Gucci, and Walmart clothes. We continue our walk and go into a furniture store; I am curious to see what he likes and does not like.

We look around for a while, settling on beautiful burl-wood living room furniture with soft ranch leather, along with a pair of mountain style lodge chairs, free form arms, buffalo hide upholstery. Five thousand for the pair, two thousand for matching ottomans. We both love them, and I call over the designer and give him my AmEx. I explain that everything will need to be held pending a new address, but that delivery will be to Twin Lakes. Taylor is astonished and when we are finished, he hugs me. "Time to go home with my soon-to-be overly rich wife."

Returning to the condo, I pick up a packet of papers on the counter. Surprised, I read an offer for the condo: $2.8 million, all cash, thirty-day close, no contingencies. A nice offer, but a thirty-day close is too fast, so I call my realtor and ask her to propose a forty-five-day close and HOA acceptance. I hang up and turn to Taylor, "You are getting richer every day."

He frowns. "This is all happening so fast. I could have killed you the other day."

"Yes, you could have," I agree, "but you didn't. You regained control because you love me."

"But Annie, I had to kill my family. That is in me."

"No, not anymore, Taylor." I look at him. "I stripped that from you. I am your family now and we can add a puppy in the months to come. Something female, soft and warm. No spay so we can have a litter of fluff balls, running around and peeing on my Persian rug."

He hugs and kisses me, leading me to the bedroom. We make love, and then make love again, our hearts growing every day as we learn our limits.

We spend a few more days in Aspen and send the signed contract via FedEx to my realtor. We drive to Twin Lakes for Taylor's appointments. Patients await, and I'm curious as Taylor explains the process to neuter, to castrate, his male patients. Cruel, but positive results and less aggression. I do notice that he shifts as he explains; few males would look forward to it.

I learn a lot during the week and Taylor is pleased to have my help. I get a little wobbly when he slits open a cow and removes a calf. The large calf takes its first breath and for a brief moment, I sadly consider that I will never have a child, only able to experience this miracle in the animal kingdom.

We stay at Tova's, who is busy organizing our wedding. Taylor can't stay at his home, the memories still too close at hand. The realtor had contacted him, and he is anxious to leave an old life. Tova has news for us as we sit down to another of her delicious dinners one evening. There is a ranch for sale, three bedrooms and two baths, lots of land and a very large barn that could be used for Taylor's practice. A large garage, rose and vegetable gardens, and we can see it tomorrow. The owner is looking to do a quick sale as his wife is in a nursing home in Denver.

"I've seen it, Annie," Tova enthuses, "and I think you would both love it, plus, it's zoned commercial for your practice, Taylor." He hugs Tova, then me as he sits back down. We enjoy a prime rib dinner and dream of our new life.

We visit the ranch in the morning, noting all the wildflowers and spruce trees, and the handsome timber frame house. I already love the deck surrounding the house and the distant view of Mount Elbert's snow-covered peaks.

We tour the house, noting the changes that would need to be made to the kitchen and baths. There are two large wood-burning fireplaces, great piles of wood already chopped and stacked on the deck. Taylor smiles and we walk out to the garage; inside are generous storage cabinets, a snowmobile, and a mover with a snow blade. The barn is huge, with an open area in front, poured concrete floors, two-twenty power, a large restroom, utilitarian kitchen and eight windowed horse stalls. Taylor seems really pleased and says, "This could work really well for my practice."

Tova says, "The only thing is, the owner wants a million dollars for it."

I smile, telling her we will take it and that I'll have the re-altor send over the contract. Tova and I agree to meet in the morning, as she also has some wedding details to go over. Just like that, our future again expands.

CHAPTER ELEVEN

Tova, Taylor, and I meet over a breakfast of Spanish omelets and fresh orange juice to discuss the wedding. She has the minister for us, menu planned, reception, flowers and cake taken care of, and she's reserved the Aspen suite for three days. I give her the list of our email contacts, along with a check for twenty-five thousand dollars to cover all the expenses. Shocked, Tova says, "This is way too much," but I stop her protest.

"You are worth every penny, Tova; you've made all of this so easy for us."

She turns to Taylor and says, "Wolf, you lost your family and found a new one." He turns away to wipe a tear.

I call a moving company to arrange for packers, our move date still unknown. Looking around Taylor's office, I realize just how big of a job this move will be. X-ray machine, computers, printers, microscopes, incubators, exam tables. So much to do, but I feel a surge of pride for my soon-to-be husband. Taylor decides to restrict his practice for the next thirty days, emergencies only, considering all we have to get done.

We return to the suite and spend a quiet afternoon pleasing each other. Taylor smiles when he sees me naked on the bed, knees raised. He opens a nearby drawer and pulls out a towel, placing it underneath me, his hands quickly bringing me pleasure, which I return with my mouth.

Later, I take a few blue tablets and we drive back to Aspen, where paperwork and chores await us. I leave Taylor with his laptop and ask him to give me some private time. He smiles at my request, telling me to take as long as I need. We have a light lunch and retreat to the bedroom, where a hot bath and our bed beckon us. I lay down and raise my knees, Taylor smiling as he says, "Again, Annie?" and I nod. He slips a towel under me, spreads oil over his hands and strokes me. I pull his hand back and slide it between the cheeks of my ass, stopping at the end and leaving it in place.

It's all the invitation Taylor needs. "Are you sure, Annie?"

I nod as I roll over and get up on my knees. Taylor runs his hand down between my buttocks and slowly, gently, fills me. "I'm going to move, baby. You are so tight; I won't last long." He slides in and out, bringing a hand from my hip to proximity.

Pushing back, I tell him, "Harder, baby."

He increases speed and jerks through his climax. "Jesus Christ, Annie, that was so good!" We both collapse on the bed.

He moves to get up, but I stop him. "No, stay on me. I want your weight." He wraps his arms around me and rests his hand on my shoulder. Suddenly, I jerk beneath him when a strong cramp seizes my thigh muscle.

"What is it, Annie?" Taylor looks alarmed.

"Leg cramp!" I sob, and I run to the shower, desperate for the hot water to massage the cramp away. Taylor joins me and drops to his knees, massaging my thigh. He squirts body wash and massages everything below my waist. My thigh muscle starts to relax, and I step out of the shower. As soon as I put weight on my leg, the cramp returns, so Taylor picks me up and carries me to the bed. He grabs oil and spreads my legs, placing one over his shoulder and firmly rolling his hands over the hard mass continuing to torture me.

"Damn it, I can't get it to soften!" Taylor says.

"Please," I beg, "just keep trying; it hurts like hell!"

Taylor increases pressure, rolling my thigh, and he's sweating and breathing heavily, until the cramp finally starts to go away. He props a pillow under me and gently lowers my leg. "Try not to move, Annie, and try not to flex your toes," he instructs. He covers me with blankets, kisses me and tells me to go to sleep. "I love you, baby. Close your eyes and take a nap; I'll work in here close to you if you need anything."

I sleep for a few hours and Taylor hands me some iced water and two Tylenol when I wake. Looking at me, he says, "Okay, I want you to get up and walk a little bit. Doctor's orders."

I get up and Taylor drops to massage my thigh. "I don't understand; I haven't had leg cramps since high school."

Taylor chuckles and says, "Well, you were in an awkward position, getting me too excited to be gentle with you, and your muscles strained." He kisses me, smacks my ass, and commands, "Clothes. Sneakers. I thought we could drive over to the ranch and walk the property."

Agreeing to the idea, we drive over to the ranch, park and walk to the back. Trees, wildflowers and a path visible out to the property line. A strange array marked with flags draws my attention. Taylor follows my gaze, noting that area is the septic tank, and we walk along the path, stopping frequently to smell the wildflowers. It is a sharp contrast to the pack's territory of barren dirt and a few bushes! I look over and I think Taylor's thoughts are running along the same lines. He is silent and seems unhappy. I kiss him and murmur, "I know you miss them."

He drops to his knees. "I need to sit, Annie." I sit down with him and draw his head to my shoulder. He quietly cries and softly admits that yes, he does miss his pack.

"I know, baby, I know," trying to soothe him. It will pass with time, but you can cry anytime you need to."

I hug him tighter and he lets out his breath. "I hate that I'm such a baby. Forty-three years old and crying like a five-year-old."

"Taylor, it's just your body telling you that you care, that you remember."

"I love you, Annie; you put up with my faults."

"They are not faults, Taylor. They are many of your signs to me of your gentle spirit." I stand up and reach my hand to him. "I want my future husband happy."

Back at the Aspen suite, I have a note from Tova; there is a FedEx package at the desk for me. I will go through it later. Right now, Taylor is my priority.

We take a quick shower, my skin telling me that I need moisturizer. We dry off and Taylor slathers the scent of gardenia on me. He then lays down on his back, and I crawl between his legs, kissing his member. He grabs my head, forcing himself deeper in my throat. "Suck me, baby, suck me," he begs, and I draw him in and out, flicking my tongue over his sensitive tip. "Christ, Annie, don't stop, I'm close!"

I answer with my mouth and he soon shudders through a strong climax. He pulls me up and kisses me. "Ugh, I hate the taste of me. How can you stand it?"

"Oh, Taylor," I say. "It is called love. I cherish watching your reactions to my pleasuring you."

We stroke each other until his body can respond again and make gentle love. After a short nap, I pick up the FedEx package, real estate contracts and papers. I notice the absence of Taylor's name, so I will have to get it added. The appraisals of my condo and two houses, as well as our new property, have all come in more generous than I thought. I have been lucky.

CHAPTER TWELVE

We have an early dinner and pack for Aspen. I need to be there for the movers and to talk to the realtor. The next day, I am busy directing the crew on what to pack and how to label it. I decide to donate some of my furniture and have them mark it as such. Taylor goes out to run some errands, so I take a little time to write ideas for wedding vows. My first attempt is too long, too revealing. He would turn to jelly and I would probably be unable to tell him.

"Taylor, I promise to love you. To cherish and support you. To guide you, to grow old with you, and face all challenges to our health. You are my life, my heartbeat, my alpha."

Much better vow: now it says what I need it to say. I am already crying just thinking about it. When Taylor walks in, he sees my tears and pulls my lips to his. "Hey, you've been crying, baby. What is wrong?"

"Nothing, Taylor; I was just writing my wedding vows."

"Oh, shit, Annie, I need to do the same." He wanders through the condo, noticing the items to donate. "Annie, I would like to have a few of these pieces for the practice. My clients have never had so much luxury as this. And I can donate almost everything from my house. I know several families we can help. I already donate a lot of no-charge services to a lot of people; I can't stand to turn away any animal in need."

"Stop, Taylor, you will make me cry again! I love you so much."

We are busy and stressed the last few days before the wedding. Taylor has had several emergencies at the practice: broken legs, attacks, injuries from accidents, and even a desperate plea from a family with puppies that had been sprayed by a porcupine.

I go with him to help with the puppies as it is two in the morning and the puppies are screaming for help. We pull the sharp quills from their cute little faces, allowing them to eat again. Handing pain medication for them over to the owner, we drive back to Aspen, missing our bed. We sleep for eight precious hours, leaving tasks undone.

The wedding is now only forty-eight hours away, so we pack what we need, close the condo and drive to Twin Lakes. Tova is excited as she shows us the venue, flowers, donations and guest estimates. The venue will be full; so many of Taylor's clients wishing him well in his new life.

We wake up the day of the wedding in each other's arms.

"Good morning, Mrs. Taylor."

"Good morning, Dr. Taylor."

We shower and have coffee, declining breakfast downstairs because we know Tova will have a feast for us. We are both dressed in white shirts open at the neck, pressed jeans and soft, brown chukka boots. I pay extra attention to my hair and make-up, Taylor just needing a smooth shave. I thread my fingers through his hair, joking that he seems to have a few new gray hairs.

"That's because you age me, Annie," He smiles.

I laugh and swat his tight ass, his jeans molded to his body.

We make our way down and hear soft violin music; a few of the volunteer firefighters are also gifted musicians. I try to hold back the emotion, knowing I must get through the upcoming vows. Everyone takes their places and the minister welcomes the large crowd, then begins.

"Do you, Edward Wolf Taylor, take this woman, Annie Jane Jacobs, to love, protect, and honor, in sickness and in health, for as long as you both shall live?"

Taylor is visibly shaking as the minister continues. Soon, he is asking for the rings and we've arrived at our own, personal vows. Taylor begins.

"Annie, with this ring I promise to love, cherish and protect you. You are my reason to live, my soul, and the reason my heart beats. I will love you forever."

"Taylor, I promise to love, to cherish and support you, to guide you and grow old with you, and face all challenges to our health. You are my life, my heartbeat, my alpha."

Taylor is struggling to control his emotion, but he can't. Tears run down his face, and down mine, as well. He wobbles a bit, so I kiss him and hold him steady. The minister declares, "You may now kiss the bride," winks, and says it again. Taylor kisses me passionately and clings to me, murmuring my name over and over. The minister announces, "Mr. and Mrs. Wolf Taylor, I now pronounce you man and wife."

I whisper to Taylor, "Are you going to faint?"

He smiles and says, "I hope not, but keep holding me up, Mrs. Taylor."

Everyone is clapping and laughing as we make our way down the aisle and into the crowd. I immediately start to hear our well-wishers telling stories about how Taylor helped them, how he refused payment, how he came out at three in the morning and saved a dog, a calf, a foal. He is the best man and I smile at these stories, as I admire him so. I am staggered at the outpouring of gratitude and praise for Taylor, and I watch as he shakes hands, hugs, and even occasionally kisses a cheek. I have evidently married a local god, and as I search for him in the crowd, I sense that he is doing the same.

Tova raises her glass. "Please enjoy this joyous day and

the start of a new life for two of my favorite people. I see a lot of tears out there and I'm about to join you. Please, eat, enough for all!"

Several men in camouflage follow Tova's lead and get up to speak to the crowd. "As most of you know, Wolf is a generous steward to the forest service and the Department of Wildlife. He has saved and rescued hundreds of eagles, deer, elk, bear, cougars, the list is endless. We are so proud of his service to us and to the animals we have been able to return to the wild. Many of you may know of, but perhaps have never witnessed, this man's intense love of wolves. His unique understanding of the breed, and his ability to talk to them. Recently, Wolf suffered a great tragedy when the pack he loved and cared for contracted a dangerous virus and had to be shot and killed. We grieve with him and want to present him with a tribute to his love for the wolf."

I clutch Taylor tightly, silently encouraging him to hold it together as more camo shirts enter the stage, carrying a large, beautifully carved wood sculpture of a wolf. "A memory of your past, Wolf, and a hope for your future. We love you, Wolf."

Taylor totally breaks down, unable to talk as tears and shudders rack his whole body. I crush him to me and turn to the crowd. "Taylor is unable to thank you all at this moment. The loss of the pack, his only family, was an earth-shattering tearing of his soul. I, along with many of you, have witnessed his gentle love and care of wolves. He could snarl, nuzzle their necks, read their aggression and fear. He was truly the leader, the alpha, and now, he is my alpha."

I see the love, tears and sorrow all directed at the man by my side. I hold him tightly to me and whisper, "Hush, hush, my love. You cannot share your pain with them, but you can share it with me tonight." I wipe his tears and he straightens his shoulders. He tries to speak but he can't get it out, so I become his voice again and thank everyone. "Taylor is embarrassed and ashamed that you had to witness this baring of his soul. Now please, go eat. Tova has worked so hard for this day; she is such a treasure to Twin Lakes."

The crowd breaks up and I take Taylor's hand, and we go sit down at one of the tables. A few minutes alone and Taylor says, "Christ, baby, I can't believe it happened again. Thank you so much for talking with them since I just couldn't. You are the bravest, most understanding woman in the world."

A few camo shirts come over and slap him on the back. "You okay, buddy?"

"Yeah, just ashamed I had to cry like a fucking baby in front of everyone."

"We loved it, Wolf. Something to tease you about next time we bring you an animal."

Taylor smiles and says, "Fuck you guys."

I pull him to another table, and we eat an elk burger. Then I wrap my arms around his waist as we stand, and I excuse us from the party so that we can go to the B & B and make love. "Thank God for you, Annie, Thank God," I hear as we pass through our guests. More hugs, pats and kisses, and I realize that I need to get Taylor out of here now. We hurry to the B & B and head up the stairs. In our suite, Taylor is still out of it, so I undress him and remove my clothes as well. I turn on the hot water for the shower and we step in, me hugging Taylor tightly as we stand under the shower. He kisses my shoulder and whispers, "I don't know what is wrong with me. I can't handle these breakdowns."

"Yes, you can, Taylor. You need one more. One more chance to release the past and dream of our future. Today is our wedding day, and your wife wants you to be happy. And" I wink, "to make me happy."

He listlessly reaches out to play with my breast and I pull his hand away, kiss him and tell him, "No, Taylor, I want you really to face that deepest part of you. You need to give up your pain, your vision of Katana being shot in the head, the look of the females and your replacement by the male, just before he was shot to death. See it, feel it, give it to me."

Taylor is crying, sobbing loudly, and I continue. "Give it to me, Taylor. Tell me, how did you feel watching the blood spurt down from their heads when their lives ended?"

"Fuck, Annie, you're hurting me."

"Good, Taylor. Good. I need you to tell me. Lash out at me until the anger and the self-hate because you had to kill them is gone."

I'm suddenly startled when he sinks his teeth into my shoulder, biting with such great force, then doing the same thing to my other shoulder, blood running freely. I turn my head and he clamps down on my neck. I whisper to him, "Go ahead. Bite me. Kill me if you need to. It will only add to your hate, but if you need to, I am here for you."

He screams, "Fuck, Annie! I can't kill you!"

"Why, Taylor?" I taunt. "Easier than a bullet to my brain."

"Because I love you, Annie!" he shouts. "Because I love you!"

"Exactly, Taylor! And that's why you can get beyond this! You loved the pack. You loved it, but they didn't love you. They let you into their world. You were their food source, so they tolerated you. You took their submission as love for you."

"Annie," Taylor protests, "I was their alpha."

"No, Taylor, you weren't. You perceived yourself as alpha, but – and listen closely here – you were never their alpha. Because the pack controlled you; you were their food source. You are lucky that they never attacked you – human prey. Can you understand, Taylor? They allowed you to get close, knowing they could kill you someday."

"No, Annie, you're wrong," Taylor says quietly.

"Taylor. You are a human. Not a wolf, and not an alpha, but a submissive to the pack. Bite me again if you need to dominate but please realize you never controlled them. They controlled you. The pack is the alpha, the true alpha. You never were. You are human, and they are wild animals, preying on your fear and misguided judgement. Think about it, Taylor. Submit to the truth. You are not, and never were, an alpha to the pack. They were the alpha, allowing a human to feed them. You are human, the wolves, wild animals. You perceived them as human, as your family, but they were never anything more than what they were – animals. The two species can learn from each other, but never mix, as nature rules. Now, cry it out, Taylor, and then end this."

He responds with huge, gulping sobs, hard tears, and a bone crushing hug. "Annie, Annie, Annie." His nose is running, his eyes overflowing, but I think he has finally accepted the message. He shudders and quivers for several long moments and sinks to the floor. I crawl to his lap, kiss him and wipe his eyes. Taylor realizes that the blood is still pouring from my bites, and he looks closely at the wounds he has inflicted.

"Fuck! Fuck! I could have killed you, Annie! Why did you let me do this?"

"Because I love you, Taylor, and I needed you to understand the truth. I trusted you to get the message before you killed me. You are human, and I love you."

He kisses me fiercely and goes to get a few things to stop the bleeding. He pulls a towel around his waist and returns with his medical bag. He leans into the shower, turning the now-cold water off, and gently lifts me out, setting me down on the edge of the tub. He applies pressure to both shoulders

Katherine Zartman

and leaves it in place. Shaking his head, he says, "You married an animal, Annie."

"No, Taylor," I assure him, "I married a wonderful, confused, but very human doctor. If you hurry up, I want to witness that."

He laughs and I breathe deeply as he lifts the towels. "Tova is going to freak over this!"

"Don't worry, Taylor. I'll tell her that I slipped and fell in the shower and you took care of me."

"I'm so sorry, Annie, but I'm going to have to stitch these wounds closed," he says sadly. I tell him to go ahead and that I'm not afraid of needles, to which he responds, "Christ, Annie, you're not afraid of anything." He pulls a syringe from his bag, along with a vial of lidocaine to numb the shoulders while he stitches the wounds. "I don't have the best gauge suture material here, so you will scar."

"It's okay, Taylor. Battle scars from my win," I smile.

He gently stitches the wounds shut with thick, black sutures; it is uncomfortable as the skin is thin on my shoulders. When he is done, he asks, "Annie? Why today? Why did this have to happen today, our wedding day?"

I take his hand. "I have been waiting months for this opportunity, and today you were so filled with raw emotion that it was the perfect time to bring the truth to you and end your conflicts with it. Today we were bonded together as two humans, no wolf. I love you."

He applies antibiotic cream and gauze bandages to my shoulders, then picks me up again and lays me in bed. Pulling the covers over me, Taylor kisses my forehead and tells me to sleep. I look at him and say, "Taylor, it is our wedding night."

He smiles. "Sleep for a few hours and I'll wake you for sex."

"Okay," I tell him. "Just don't wait too long."

I close my eyes, anxiety and exhaustion forcing them to

62

stay closed. I wake around one a.m., and see that Taylor is naked, asleep beside me, his arm around my waist and his leg between mine. He shifts. "How are you feeling, Mrs. Taylor?"

I raise my hips and he kisses me deeply, running his hands down my body. He sucks on my breasts and gently places fingers in me. I tell him to take me hard, but he says, "No, Annie. I need to be gentle right now. To love you and worship you, my wife."

He enters me and slowly makes love to me. He climaxes silently and I take his head in my hands, his green eyes staring right into my soul.

"Taylor, I promise to love you, to cherish you, to support you, guide you and grow old with you, and face challenges of health the future may hold. You are my life, my heartbeat, my..."

He interrupts and whispers, "Alpha."

"No, Taylor, the alpha is gone. Only you remain."